D1298088

Wolf Plays Alone

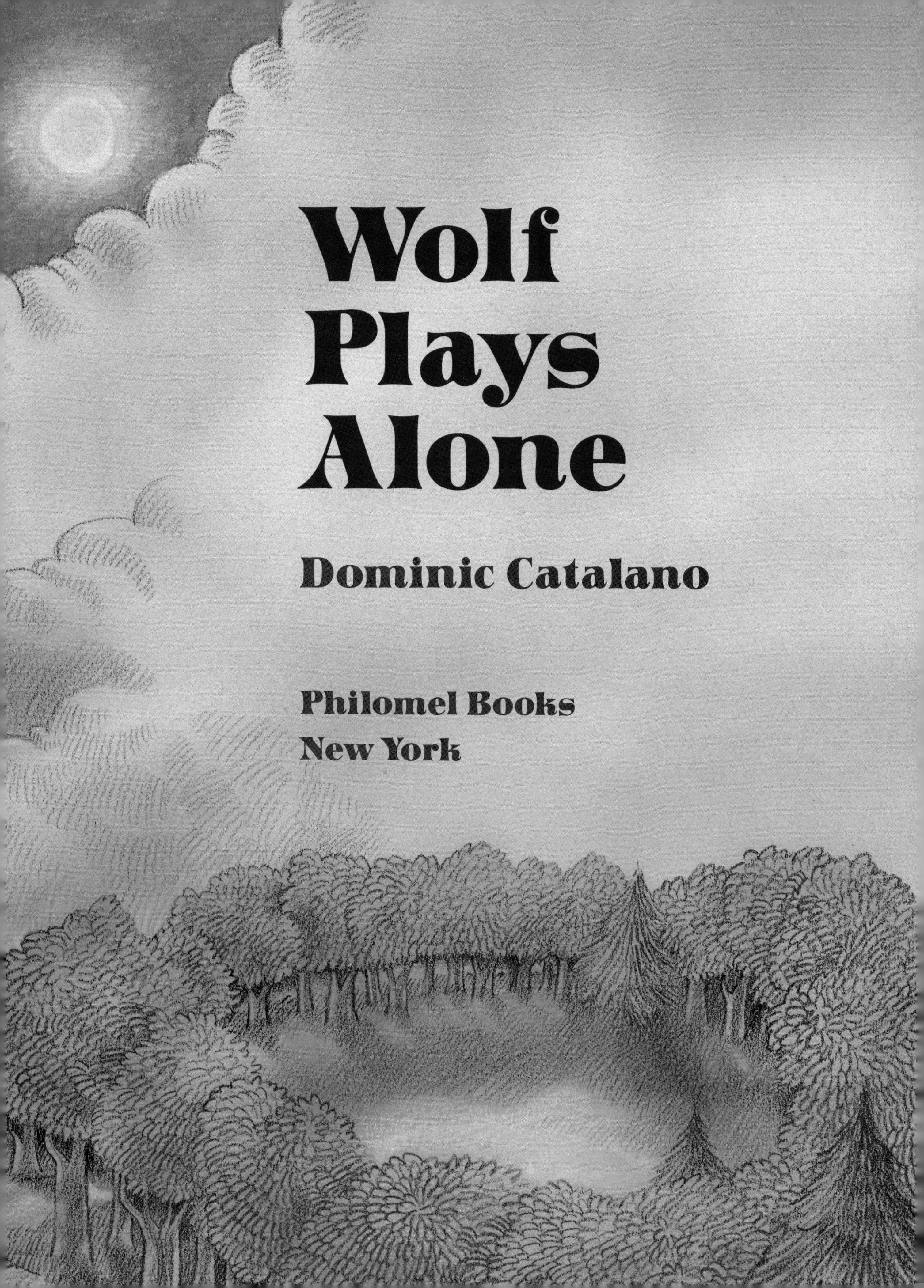

Wolf Plays Alone

Dominic Catalano

Philomel Books
New York

For Ginny

In the wood there's a clearing,
a moon-bright clearing,
where animals come
to play.

And in that clearing
stands a wolf.
He raises his horn
to play a tune
alone.

Suddenly...

Enter the rabbits
squeaking off-key
as the wolf with a horn
tries to play his tune
alone.

Enter the bear
who pounds the drum
louder than the rabbits
squeaking off-key
as the wolf with a horn
tries to play his tune
alone.

Enter the fox
who squeezes a box
faster than the bear
who pounds too loud
as the rabbits squeak
and the wolf with a horn
tries to play his tune
alone.

Enter the birds
who screech and squawk
higher than the fox
squeezing a box
as the bear pounds
as the rabbits squeak
and the wolf with a horn
tries to play his tune
alone.

Enter the moose
who blows too loose
lower than the birds
who screech and squawk
as the fox squeezes
as the bear pounds
as the rabbits squeak
and the wolf with a horn
tries to play his tune
alone.

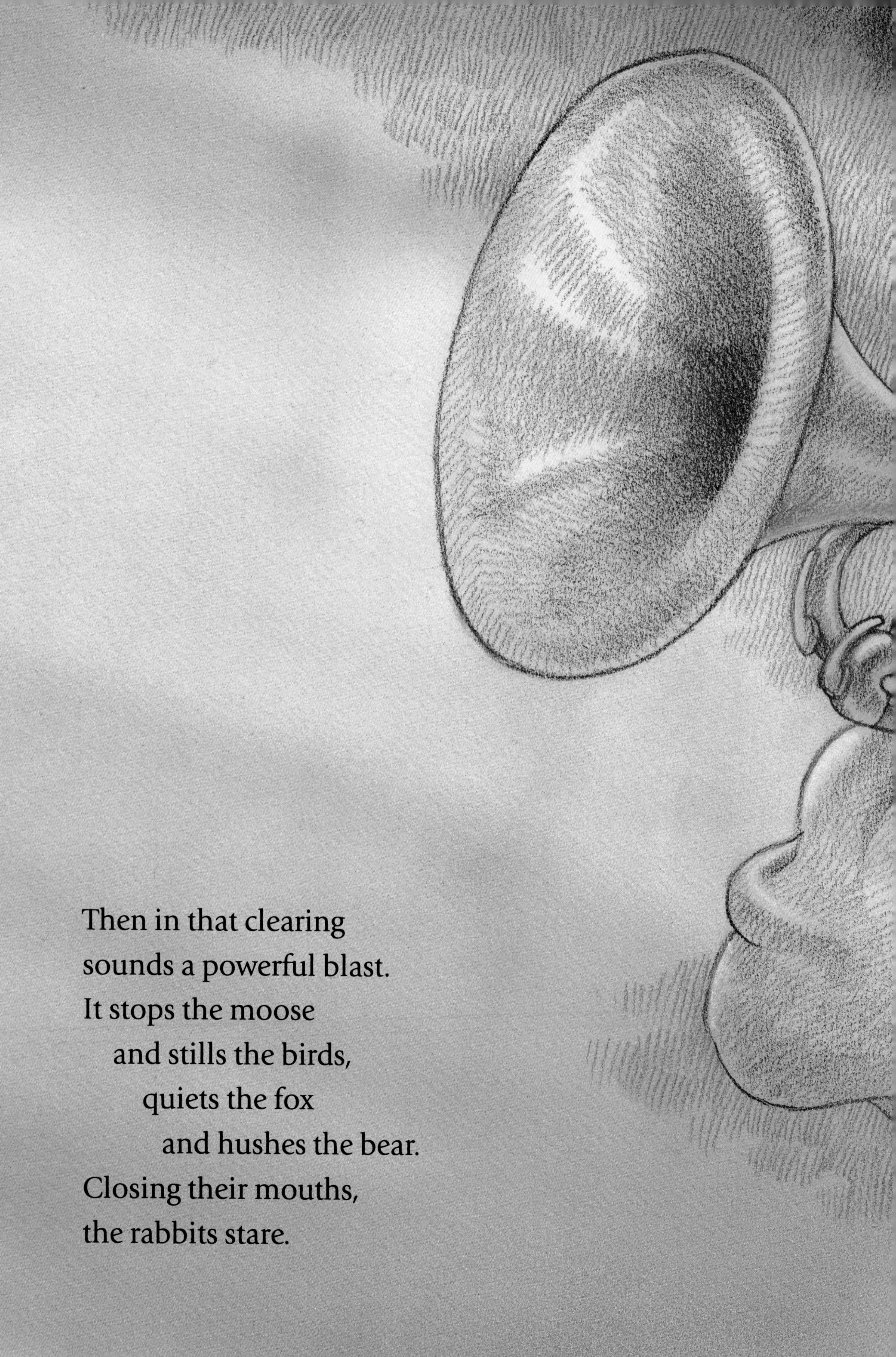

Then in that clearing
sounds a powerful blast.
It stops the moose
    and stills the birds,
        quiets the fox
            and hushes the bear.
Closing their mouths,
the rabbits stare.

Out steps the wolf
and with a wave of his arm
a music is born
as the animals play...

together.

Exit the moose,
how low he blew.
Exit the birds,
how high their sound.
Exit the fox,
how lush her chords.
Exit the bear,
how catchy his beat,

and exit the rabbits,
how sweet was their song.

All are gone…

but the wolf in the wood.
In a moon-bright clearing,
he raises his horn...

to play his tune alone.

 Philomel Books, a division of The Putnam & Grosset Book Group,
200 Madison Avenue, New York, NY 10016. Published simultaneously in Canada.
Printed in Hong Kong by South China Printing Co. (1988) Ltd. The text is set in Giovanni. Book design by Gunta Alexander.
The artist used pastel, colored pencil and watercolor paints to create the illustrations for this book.
The art was then color separated by laser and reproduced in full color.
Library of Congress Cataloging-in-Publication Data
Catalano, Dominic. Wolf plays alone / written and illustrated by Dominic Catalano. p. cm.
Summary: A wolf who wants to play his horn alone in the woods is joined by one noisy animal after another.
[1. Wolves—Fiction. 2. Animals—Fiction. 3. Music—Fiction.] I. Title. PZ7.C268777Wo 1992 [E]—dc20 91-31276 CIP AC
ISBN 0-399-21868-8
1 3 5 7 9 10 8 6 4 2
First Impression